Little Tom Meets Mr. Jonah

By PHILIP DALE SMITH

and PAT DAY-BIVINS

Illustrated by
DONNA BROOKS

Golden
Anchor
Press

Tacoma, Washington

THIS BOOK IS DEDICATED

To Reg and Jo Rhoads, my marvelous brother and super-special sister-in-law; with gratitude for the way you have touched my life and the lives of so many others, especially children and youth. --Philip Dale Smith

To the following, with much love: My brother, James T. Day; my sister-in-law, Marjorie Day; my niece, Linda Castleberry; my great-nephews, Mitchell and Ryan; and my grand-niece, Taryn. You are special! --Pat Day-Bivins

To all who feel unworthy and without hope: May this book encourage you to go to God's Word. There you'll find that all through the ages He has been the God of second chances. He still is. --Donna Brooks

Publisher's Cataloging-in-Publication
(Provided by Quality Books, Inc.)

Smith, Philip Dale
 Little Tom meets Mr. Jonah / written by Philip Dale Smith and Pat Day-Bivins ; illustrated by Donna Brooks --1st ed.
  p. cm..
  LCCN: 99-95496
  ISBN: 1-886864-16-0
  SUMMARY: In Old Testament times, a kitten named Little Tom disobeys his father's orders to avoid the fishing dock, and finds himself aboard a ship with the prophet Jonah.

  1. Jonah (Biblical prophet)--Juvenile fiction.
2. Kittens--Juvenile fiction. I. Day-Bivins, II. Brooks, Donna III. Title.

PZ7.S64465Li 2000   [E]
      QBI99-1227

Published by Golden Anchor Press
1801 S. 112th St., Tacoma, WA 98444
Printed in Hong Kong by C&C Offset

Copyright © 2000 by
Philip Dale Smith and Pat Day-Bivins
Illustrations © 2000 by Donna Brooks

The art for each picture is an original oil painting on canvas, which is color-separated and reproduced in full color.

This book is printed on acid-free paper
(So your children can pass it on to their children)

THANK YOU
We express our gratitude to school children across the nation who sent pictures of cats to the artist and who suggested names for the mean old cat. Congratulations to Muhlenberg County Christian Academy in Central City, Ky. for submitting "Claws," the name chosen for the cat. Schools that are interested in being a part of future children's book projects may contact the publisher at Post Office Box 45208, Tacoma, WA 98445

Cover design by Foster and Foster
Fairfield, Iowa

Golden Anchor books are available at special discount for bulk purchases for fund-raising efforts, sales promotions, and educational use. Special editions, excerpts, prints, etc, can be created to specification.

Little Tom pounced on his smallest sister from behind a basket. She went sprawling.

"You had better watch out for me!"
Little Tom told his three sisters. "I'm big and I'm tough!" he bragged. He had teased them all morning.

3

"Little Tom," said his father, "I've told you and told you not to be rough with your sisters. Your mother planned to take all of you to hunt mice. Since you were bad, you can't go. Instead, I'll send you to guard the wheat storage bin near the Joppa boat dock."

"Let me go hunting, Dad. I'll be good," begged Little Tom.

"You've promised before, but you didn't keep your promises. Go guard the wheat. Show me you can obey," said Dad. "And don't stop at the dock. You'll get into trouble by eating someone else's fish. Go directly to the wheat bin."

"Aw, Dad," said Little Tom, "Do I have to?"

"Yes, Son, but be back by dark. And stay away from the dock."

4

Little Tom frowned as he poked along toward the wheat bin. *Boring. Boring! BORING! Dad has already caught all the mice and rats at the wheat bin. I'll be soooooooo bored.*

When Little Tom came to the dock he stopped. *No one believes I'm big and tough,* he thought. *But I am! They think I'll get in trouble, but I won't. I'll show them!*

5

He strutted onto the dock. *Look at all the boats. And look at that interesting box. I'll bet it has fish in it. It won't hurt to look at the fish. I'm big and I'm tough and I'll just look at the fish. I won't eat any.*

6

He climbed up and peeked in.
Wow! What a big box of fish.

It won't hurt to climb in with the fish, he thought. And he did.

7

It won't hurt to take one big sniff of the fish, he thought. And he did. SNIFFFF! They smelled wonderful!

8

It won't hurt to lick the fish, Little Tom
told himself. And he did. SLURRRRRP!
It was so good!

9

It won't hurt to take one tiny bite under the fin. No one will ever notice. And he did. UMMMMMMMM! Just delicious!

10

Munch, munch, munch, munch, munch! Little Tom stuffed his belly full of fish. That made him so sleepy. He just had to take a catnap.

11

BANG! Someone slammed a top on the box!
They picked up the box. *Where were they
taking him?* Thud! They dropped the
box. It landed hard. Little Tom waited.
Then he pushed on the top.
It wouldn't move!

He pushed the top as hard as he could. It moved a little.
Then it moved more. Soon he stuck his head out.

He was on a ship going out to sea! There was water all around! What could he do?

Little Tom climbed out of the
box. Someone was coming!
He tried to hide.

14

Just then the ship's cook and a big, ugly cat hurried over to the box. "Who's been eating my fish?" bellowed the cook. "There's cat hair on my fish!"

15

"Look, Claws!" said the cook to the big cat, "Get that kitten."
Little Tom fled across the deck. He sped around the corner
and scurried up the first thing he came to—a man!
16

The surprised man stared down at the trembling kitty clinging to him. "Hi, little fellow," he said. He cuddled the scared kitten in his hands just as the cook's big cat skidded to a halt right in front of them.

17

"Scat, Claws!" the passenger yelled. He stomped his foot, and the big cat scampered away.

The man stroked the kitten gently. "I don't know your name," he said, "but I'll call you 'Little Traveler,' because a traveler is what you are. My name is Mr. Jonah. Let's go below deck and get some rest.

"God told me to go to Nineveh," Jonah told Little Tom, as the kitten snuggled with him on his bunk. "But I don't like that city and its people. So I'm going the other way as far as I can. I'll bet you're a runaway, too. You stay close to me. I'll take care of you."

Little Tom purred contentedly. *Maybe I'm not in such bad trouble after all*, he thought. They were soon sound asleep.

But during the night a terrible storm arose. The captain shouted from the top of the stairs, "Wake up, Jonah! The ship is about to sink. Pray to your God that we may be saved!"

19

Jonah sprang up. "I should have known I couldn't run away from God." He rushed to the deck. Little Tom bounded up the steps behind him. "It's my fault," Jonah told the sailors. "Throw me into the sea. Perhaps God will give you a chance to escape with your lives."

20

Little Tom watched from on top the empty fish box.
He could hardly believe his eyes! The sailors picked
up Mr. Jonah and hurled him into the swirling water.

Just then an enormous wave hit the ship. Over the side tumbled
the box. Down went the kitty with it! Little Tom plunged beneath
a huge wave and came sputtering to the surface.

21

Floating right beside him was the box! He climbed in and shook himself off. *Oh! How I hate being wet!* he thought.

He saw Mr. Jonah swimming toward him. Suddenly a monstrous fish appeared behind the man. Little Tom meowed, "Look out!" but the huge fish swallowed his friend with one gulp! Right then the storm stopped.

23

Little Tom looked at his box. *This box is a good boat*, he thought. *But I don't want to be in a boat. I want to go home! Why did I disobey and go to the dock? Why did I take someone else's fish? If only I had been good. If only poor Mr. Jonah hadn't disobeyed God and tried to run away. If only we could have a second chance.*

24

That night he curled up in the corner of the box and went to sleep. He dreamed he was at home playing nicely with his sisters and having a wonderful time. The next morning he awoke and thought, *Oh, no! It was just a dream! I'm far, far from home.*

25

The day went on and on. The sun burned down on him. He was soon sick of bobbing about on the sea. As night came he thought, *I'm not so big, after all. I'm not so tough, either.* Again he went to sleep dreaming of home. He imagined purring gently while his mother licked his fur all over.

The next morning he awoke when the box hit something.
It was the shore! Little Tom raced up and down the beach
turning summersaults and kitty-cat cartwheels.

Then, SPLOOSH! In the distance a gigantic fish appeared.
It was the same one that swallowed Mr. Jonah. It swam right
toward the beach with its big mouth wide open!

28   The fish belched a huge belch—BURRRRRRP! Out flew Mr. Jonah! "Kerthump," he landed on the soft sand.

The happy kitty rushed to Mr. Jonah, pounced on him, and licked his hand.

Mr. Jonah said, "Oh, Little Traveler, I didn't think I'd ever see you again. But God is good! He kept me alive inside the great fish. He is the God of second chances. When we're bad, He doesn't give up. He lets us try again. He's given me a second chance to go to Nineveh. I believe He wants you to have a second chance, too. I'll help you get back to Joppa."

"Look," said Mr. Jonah, "God even made sure I didn't lose my moneybag. I have money for our trip home. You'll be able to find your family. I'll get supplies and go to Nineveh like God told me to." The next day they boarded a ship for home.

When they arrived at Joppa, Mr. Jonah stroked the kitten and said, "Go find your family, Little Traveler. God has given us a second chance. They'll also give you one."

"Meow!" said the kitty as he licked Mr. Jonah's hand. Then Little Tom hurried through the crowd.

Will Mother and Dad really give me a second chance? he wondered. *Will they remember me?* "Meow," he cried. And more loudly, "Meow, Meow, MEOW!"

Then his mother's familiar voice called from nearby, "Meow! Meow!"

30   "Mom! Dad!" They came running toward him! "I'm sorry I was bad. May I have a second chance?" he begged.

"Oh, yes!" said his mother. They licked and licked him.

"Little Tom," said Dad, "even parents need second chances."

That night Little Tom curled up with his sisters in the soft, sweet smelling hay. *I'll never forget Mr. Jonah or the lessons we learned together,* he thought as he yawned a big yawn.

God will always love me. My family will always love me. They gave me a second chance. I'm glad to know about second chances, but I'll try extra hard to be good. Little Tom purred softly as he slowly drifted off to sleep.

32